MR. GRUMBLE

by Roger Hargreaves

D0708891

PSS!
PRICE STERN SLOAN
An Imprint of Penguin Group (USA) Inc.

Mr. Grumble's name suited him well!

"Bah!" he would grumble, every morning,
when his alarm clock rang.
"It's the start of yet another horrible day!"

"Bah!" he would groan every afternoon,
on his walk in the country.
"I hate the countryside!"

One day, just after he had said this,
someone suddenly appeared by magic.

It was a wizard.

A wizard, to whom Mr. Grumble had the nerve to say, "Bah! I hate wizards who suddenly appear by magic."

"Really?" said the wizard.
"Well, I don't like people who are constantly grumbling and moaning. I'll tell you what I do to people who have bad manners.
I turn them into . . .

. . . little pigs!"

And the wizard disappeared,
leaving behind him a very piggy
looking Mr. Grumble.

Mr. Grumble was afraid that he might
remain a pig for the rest of his life.

But five minutes later,
by magic, of course,
he changed back into his old self.

He set off again and happened to pass
Little Miss Fun's house.

"Come in!" she cried.
"I'm having a party!"

Mr. Grumble went in, but when he heard
Little Miss Fun's guests singing and
laughing he scowled.

"Bah!" he moaned.
"I can't stand singing and laughing!"

He would have done better to
have kept quiet, because . . .

. . . the wizard appeared once more.

"I see that my first lesson
wasn't enough!" he said.
"If I am going to teach you to stop grumbling,
groaning and moaning, I'll have to do
more than turn you into a little pig,
I'll have to turn you into . . .

. . . a big pig!"

Mr. Grumble did not like it one bit.

Little Miss Fun and her guests, however, found it very funny.

"Please," begged Mr. Grumble,
"turn me back to normal!
I promise that I will never grumble,
groan or moan ever again!"

And he feebly wiggled his curly tail.

The wizard took pity on him
and changed him back into his old self.

And then the wizard disappeared again.

Then Little Miss Fun jumped on to a table
and pretended to be a clown.

Mr. Grumble was not amused.

"Bah!" he snorted.
"I can't stand people who jump on to tables
and pretend to be clowns!"

You can guess what happened next.

He turned into . . .

. . . an enormous pig!

An enormous pig whose face was
red with embarrassment!

"Oink!" wailed Mr. Grumble, mournfully.

Then, this enormous red-faced pig,
made a solemn promise.

"Never again will I grumble, groan
moan or snort!"

"Good," said the wizard,
suddenly appearing once again.

And Mr. Grumble changed back
into his old self!

Well, not exactly his old self!

Look at that smile on his face.

Amazing, isn't it?

Later, Mr. Grumble went home.

And, tired out after his exhausting day,
he went straight to bed.

He slept the whole night
without once grumbling,
groaning, moaning or snorting.

But not without . .

. . . snoring!